ANIMAL LORE & LEGEND

RABBIT

American Indian Legends Retold by D. L. Birchfield
Additional Text & Book Design by Vic Warren
Illustrations by Diana Magnuson

SCHOLASTIC INC.
New York Toronto London Auckland Sydney

The tradition of American Indian storytelling is older than history. The authors are proud to bring this art form to the pages of this book, in the hope that we may entertain, educate, and inspire a new generation of children.

We wish to extend our thanks to the Cherokee and Taos nations for their stories.

Library of Congress Cataloging-in-Publication Data

Birchfield, D. L.
Animal lore & legend — rabbit / American Indian legends / retold by D. L. Birchfield ; additional text & book design by Vic Warren ; illustrations by Diana Magnuson.
p. cm.
Summary: Includes both factual information and Indian legends about North American rabbits and hares.
ISBN 0-590-22490-5
1. Indians of North America — Folklore. 2. Rabbits —Folklore. 3. Rabbits — Juvenile literature. 4. Tales — North America. [1. Rabbits — Folklore. 2. Indians of North America — Folklore. 3. Rabbits.] I. Birchfield, D. L., 1948- . II. Warren, Vic, 1943- . III. Magnuson, Diana, ill., 1947- . IV. Title: Animal lore & legend — rabbit.
E98.F6A54 1995
398.24'52897'08997—dc20 94-43935
CIP
AC

12 11 10 9 8 7 6 5 4 3 2 1 6 7 8 9/9 0 1/0

Printed in the U.S.A. 09

First Scholastic printing, March 1996

Photos:

Title page, White-tailed jack rabbit

Back cover, Cottontail rabbit

D. L. Birchfield is an enrolled member of the Choctaw Nation of Oklahoma. He has been an editor and columnist for several Native American publications, including *News from Indian Country, Portland Indian News, The Raven Chronicles, Moccasin Telegraph,* and *Turtle Quarterly*. His work has appeared in several collections of essays, short stories, and poetry, and he has written two biographies for children: *Tecumseh, Leader* and *Jim Thorpe, World's Greatest Athlete*. He is currently at work as General Editor of a forthcoming 11-volume encyclopedia of American Indians.

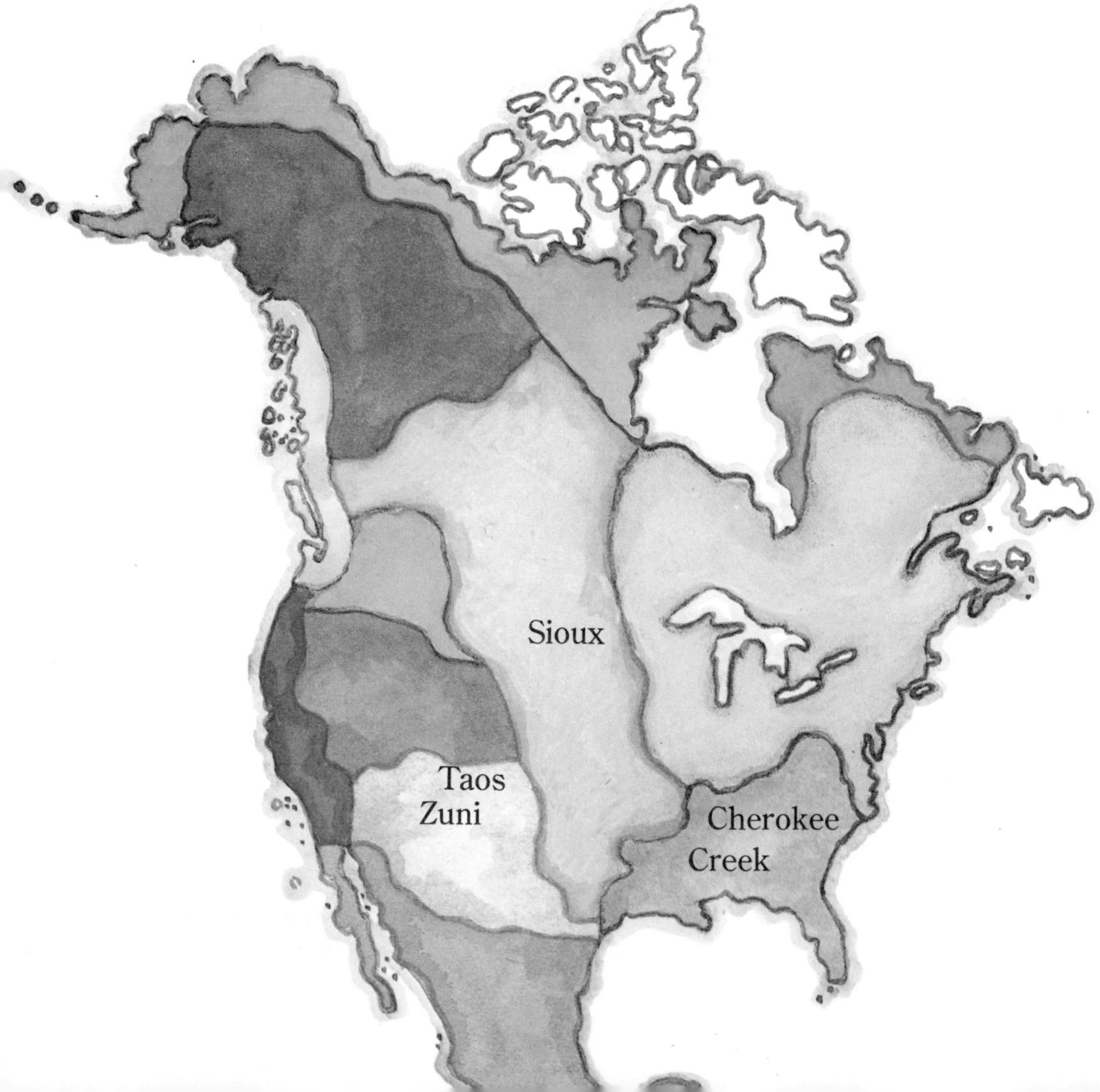

Cottontail rabbits live in most parts of North America except the Far North. They are 11 to 21 inches long.

Cottontails are named for their little white tails.

The jack rabbit is not a rabbit.
It is a hare.
Hares are bigger than rabbits.
They have bigger ears and hind legs.

Jack rabbits live in open areas of
western North America.

Black-tailed jack rabbit

Jack rabbits are about two feet long.
They have very big ears.

They have long legs made for speed.
They can leap more than 20 feet.
They can run 45 miles an hour.
Their enemies, like coyotes and
foxes, cannot run this fast.

WHY POSSUM'S TAIL IS BARE

A Cherokee Story

Rabbit wanted all the animals to
think that he was good-looking.
But he had a short, fuzzy tail.

Possum had a long, bushy tail.
It was so pretty.
Rabbit was jealous.

"Hey, Possum," said Rabbit.
"Come to the dance tonight.
I will get Cricket to comb your
pretty tail."

"Okay," said Possum.
"But first I have to take a nap."

Possum went to sleep.

“Hey, Cricket,” said Rabbit.
“Possum wants a haircut.
He wants you to trim his tail.”

“Okay,” said Cricket.
“How does he want it cut?”

“Real short,” said Rabbit.

While Possum was asleep, Cricket cut
all the hair off Possum’s tail.

Rabbit came by.
He tied a big ribbon on Possum's tail.

When Possum woke up, he said,
"Why do I have a ribbon on my tail?"

"It's a big surprise," said Rabbit.
"Don't take it off until you dance."

"Okay," said Possum.
"I like to be surprised."

That night at the dance Possum
took off the ribbon.
Then he began to dance.

The animals laughed and laughed.
Possum's tail looked so funny.

Possum looked at his tail to see what
was wrong.

When Possum saw his tail, he fainted from the big surprise.

To this day, Possum still faints every time he gets a big surprise.
And Possum's tail is still bare.

Now Rabbit says that his tail is much better looking.

A cottontail listens for danger.

To the tribes of southeastern North America, Rabbit is the trickster.
Many stories tell of Rabbit fooling other animals.

We learn from trickster tales.
We learn not to be foolish or mean.

The Creek name for Rabbit, the trickster, is "Pasikola."

Zuni rabbit fetish

Rabbits use their color
and stillness to hide.

Rabbits rest and sleep in small, shallow holes called forms. Sometimes cottontails take over old burrows left empty by badgers, skunks, prairie dogs, or foxes. Sometimes rabbits live at the bottom of piles of thick brush.

RABBIT GOES DUCK HUNTING

A Cherokee Story

Rabbit is tricky.
He likes to brag about how tricky he can be.

One day Rabbit tricked all the other animals in the forest.

Rabbit hid behind a tree.
He said, "Look at me!
Look at me!
I'm the prettiest thing
you ever did see!"

Then Rabbit ran from tree to tree.
He ran so fast that no one got
a good look at him.

"Oh, my," said Owl.
"That rabbit must be so pretty."

"He is, isn't he?" said Frog.

"I wish I could get a better look
at him," said Otter.

Rabbit just laughed and laughed.

He decided to play a big trick on Otter.
"I can catch ducks," said Rabbit.
"Just like Otter."

"This I have got to see," said Otter.

All the animals went to the river.

“This is how I do it,” said Otter.
Otter dove into the river.
He swam under a duck and caught it.
“Let’s see you do that,” said Otter.

Rabbit made a rope from some briars.
He dove in and swam to a duck.

"Hey, Duck," said Rabbit.
"How about a ride?"

"Okay," said Duck.
"Throw the rope."

Rabbit threw the rope.

Duck flapped his wings hard.
He flew away, dragging Rabbit
through the air.

"Look at me!" said Rabbit.
"I caught a duck."

"Look!" said Owl.
"Rabbit caught a duck."

"He sure did!" said Frog.

"I would not believe it," said Otter,
"but I saw it with my own eyes."

That Rabbit is tricky.
The animals say he can catch ducks.
They saw him do it.

Cottontail kits in their nest

Photo: Leonard Lee Rue III

Adult rabbits are called bucks and does.
Baby rabbits are called kits or kittens.

Mother rabbits make nests.
They dig out a bowl in the ground.
They line it with bits of their fur.
They have two to four babies.
Sometimes they have up to eight.

Cottontail kits are about four inches long when they are born.
They are born pink and hairless.
They are also blind and deaf.
In one or two weeks, they have fur.
They can also see and hear.

Baby jack rabbits are born with fur.
Their eyes are open.
They leave the nest in only three or four weeks.

Desert Southwest rabbit drawing

RABBIT AND THE TAR WOLF

From the Cherokee and Taos Stories

One summer it never did rain.
The animals had to dig a well.

Rabbit hid in a thicket and watched.

Rabbit always drank drops of dew
from the thorn bushes in the thicket.
So he was not thirsty.

Other animals could not drink that dew.
There were too many thorns.

But Rabbit needed a bath.
"I can't look nice," said Rabbit,
"if I can't take a bath."

That night Rabbit sneaked to the well.
He took a big, splashy bath.
He scrubbed himself all over.
It felt so good.

Then the animals came to get a drink.

“Somebody took a bath in our well!” said Owl.

“We can’t drink bath water!” said Frog.

“I will fix that rascal,” said Otter. He got some tar and made a tar wolf. He said, “This will do the job.”

That night Rabbit came to take a bath.
But the tar wolf was in the way.
"Step aside!" said Rabbit.
"Or I will punch you in the nose."

But the tar wolf did not move.

So Rabbit gave him a big punch
in the nose.

Rabbit got his fist stuck in the tar.

The animals all laughed when they found Rabbit stuck in the tar.

"What should we do now?" said Owl.

"Whatever you do," cried Rabbit, "don't throw me in that thicket. There is nothing in there to drink, and it is full of thorns."

“That sounds good to me,” said Otter.

Otter pulled Rabbit out of the tar.
Then he threw him in the thicket.

Rabbit just laughed and laughed.
He was back home where he belonged.
And he had lots of dew to drink.

That Rabbit is a tricky rascal.

Rabbit is quiet and soft.
We must all learn to be like that,
say the Oglala Sioux.

In the Far North, jack rabbits grow
white fur in the winter.
They dig burrows in the snow.
Two other hares live in the Far North.
They are the Arctic hare and the
snowshoe hare.

Snowshoe hare

Rabbits eat many grasses and leaves.
They can be pests to farmers.
Without predators like owls and coyotes,
there would be too many rabbits.
They would be a very big problem.
Left alone, all animals find a natural
balance that helps them all.

Arctic hare

GLOSSARY

Cherokee (chair′-o-kee): An Indian nation of southeastern North America

Creek: An Indian nation of southeastern North America

Oglala Sioux (ohg-la′-la soo): A tribal group of the Sioux nation of the Great Plains

Predator (preh′-dah-tor): A person, animal, or thing that hunts or preys on others

Taos (tah′-ose): A Pueblo nation of the desert Southwest

Trickster: The hero of many folktales from all over the world.
Many people teach their children with trickster tales.
Rabbit is only one trickster.
Other parts of the world have other tricksters, such as:

Anansi (a-non′-see), the Spider — western Africa
Coyote (ky′-ote) — southwestern North America
Monkey — Latin America and Asia
Mouse deer — Indonesia
Raven — northwestern North America
Reynard, the Fox — Europe
Turtle — northeastern North America

Zuni (zoo′-nee): A Pueblo nation of the desert Southwest